SAVING ELI'S LIBRARY

Ruth Horowitz   *illustrated by* Brittany Jackson

Albert Whitman & Company
Chicago, Illinois

ELI'S LIBRARY stood by a river
that tumbled between two mountains.

Eli loved his library.

He loved the computers,
where Josey James chatted
with her faraway sister.

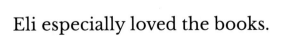

He loved to stretch with
Big Sam's yoga class and
to help Luke and Lena
play chess.

Eli especially loved the books.

On Tuesdays, the kids squished onto the braided rug to hear Miss Mudge's stories. Eli especially loved the stories with brave heroes and scary monsters.

And he loved how the river tumbled outside, like it was telling its story too.

One Tuesday, Eli and Dad drove to the library through sheets of rain. The windshield wipers slapped and swished.

The river roared like a monster from one of Miss Mudge's stories. Eli had never seen it so wild.

In the library parking lot, people were stacking sandbags.

"River's rising!" Big Sam hollered.

"Pick up the pace!" yelled Josey James.

More people were rushing
around inside.

"What about Story Circle?"
Eli asked.

"No time!" said Miss
Mudge. "We're moving
the books so the water
won't reach them."

Eli's heart pounded.
He couldn't let the
river ruin the books.

"Can we help?" he asked Dad.

Eli pulled books off the low shelves and passed them to Dad, who tucked them away on the high shelves. They worked as fast as they could while the river raged outside, singing the story of the storm.

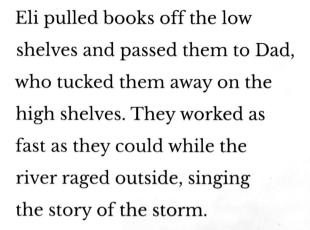

But before Eli and the others could finish, Little Sammy hollered, "River's almost over the bridge!"

"Better hurry home!" Big Sam yelled.

Eli and Dad dashed to the car through the drenching rain.

The river was roiling. The tires slipped on the steep mountain road. Rain flooded the windshield as fast as the wipers could swipe.

It was good to get home and dry off.

But Eli kept thinking about the library.
If the river wrecked it, how would Josey
James chat with her sister? Where would
the yoga class and chess players go?
And what about the books?

Miss Mudge's stories all had happy endings.
Would this one?

Worry tumbled through Eli's mind that
whole stormy night.

By morning the sun was back.
But the mountain road was sloshy.

The river was mud brown
and boiling.

The library parking lot was a lake.

The sandbags were slick with slime.

What was it like inside? Eli took Dad's hand.

The braided rug was stinky with sludge. Eli wrinkled his nose.

The lowest shelves were ruined. Eli squeezed his eyes shut.

He could hear the river roaring on and on outside, like it was bragging about what it had done.

"Quiet, you mean river!" Eli shouted.

"It could have been a lot worse," said Miss Mudge.

Eli followed her pointing finger. There, on the highest shelves, were the books they'd moved, safe and dry.

"You helped do that," said Miss Mudge. "You're a library hero."

Eli's heart pounded. But it would take more than one hero to get the library back in shape.

Then—

"I brought extra shovels!" Luke called.

"Load the trash in my truck!" Lena yelled back.

Little Sammy showed up, with Josey James right behind him.

"Can we help?" Eli asked Dad.

Tuesday was
Work Day now.

When Big Sam
shoveled sludge into
bags, Eli organized
the twist ties.

When Miss Mudge filled the new shelves,
Eli made sure the books sat straight.

And when Luke brought in a new braided
rug, Eli knew just where it belonged.

It took tons of Tuesdays and more
helpers than Eli could count.

But when they were done,

the library was
better than ever.

It seemed like the whole town came
to celebrate. There was music and cake,
and Eli got to march in a book parade.

Eli couldn't stop smiling.
Especially when the kids squished onto the new rug.

"There once was a town that saved its library," Miss Mudge's story began. She wasn't reading from a book.

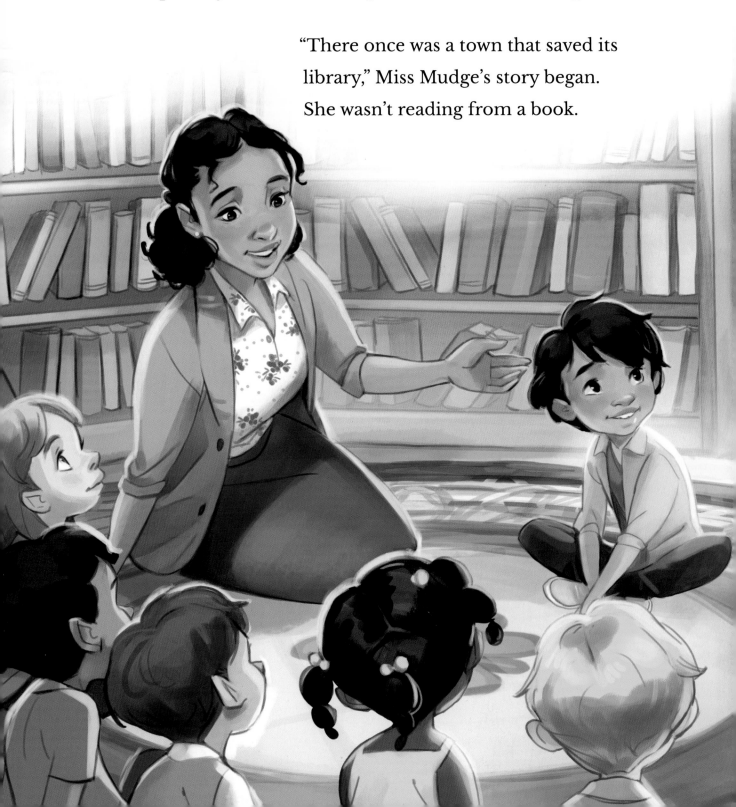

Eli looked around, his heart pounding.
Miss Mudge was talking about him
and Dad and everyone there.

And even the river tumbling
outside, telling its story too.

AUTHOR'S NOTE

This story is fiction. But it was inspired by the true story of the public library in Lincoln, Vermont. After a fire struck in 1924, the town moved the library into the basement of a new community center beside the New Haven River. When the river flooded in 1938, wiping out the entire library collection, the town rallied to replace the lost books.

In 1998 the river flooded once more. This time the only books that survived were those that were on the highest shelves or out on loan during the flood. When the town worked together yet again and built a free-standing library away from the river, those borrowed books formed the core of the new collection. To celebrate the reopening, kids pulled little red wagons filled with children's books down River Road to the books' new home.

Saving Eli's Library celebrates the enduring bigheartedness of the Lincoln community, and recognizes the capricious powers of rain and rivers.

———

In memory of Luke—RH

To Ruth—I'm so grateful the opportunity you've given me to tell Eli's story through my work.
Through this experience, I have sought and found inspiration in local libraries and bookstores,
reconnecting with old friends while making new ones over our love of books. This experience
has reminded me that libraries are where friends are made, and dreams are born through
the stories that inspire us. Libraries are places of wonder that are worth protecting.
Thank you for helping me reconnect with some of my own. —BJ

———

Library of Congress Cataloging-in-Publication data is on file with the publisher.

Text copyright © 2020 by Ruth Horowitz
Illustrations copyright © 2020 by Albert Whitman & Company
Illustrations by Brittany Jackson
First published in the United States of America in 2020 by Albert Whitman & Company
ISBN 978-0-8075-1971-4 (hardcover)
ISBN 978-0-8075-1972-1 (ebook)
Printed in China
10 9 8 7 6 5 4 3 2 1 WKT 24 23 22 21 20

Design by Aphelandra Messer

For more information about Albert Whitman & Company,
visit our website at www.albertwhitman.com.